Wonder World KiDS

THE MYSTERY OF THE DANCING HORSES

Book 1

Written by Dori Marx

Illustrated by Lisa Freidl

ISBN: 978-1-7323424-0-8

All rights reserved. Published in the United States by Noreaster Times LLC, Sandy Hook, CT.

For the real L & C & F who offer
enough inspiration for a library filled with stories...
and for P, imagine me and you, I do – D.M.

Sandy Hook School
One School One Read 2020
This Book Belongs To

_____

CHAPTER 1.

"Are we there yet?" ten-year-old Lilly Cook yawned and stretched her long legs to get more comfortable.

Her younger twin siblings Fynn and Celia looked at each other and started laughing at the same time. Although they were constantly arguing, they became perfectly agreeable when it came to making fun of their older sister.

The eight-year-olds didn't look anything alike but once you caught the same glimmer in their dark-brown eyes, you could tell that they were related.

"Lilly, we haven't even reached the airport. We left the house about 45 minutes ago," replied her mom from the passenger seat of the car.

Lilly frowned in the back seat. She had finished her cheese sandwich and apple juice box, battled some invading spiders in Minecraft, looked out of the window at the landscape zipping by, and was ready for the vacation to begin now.

Sure, it was amazing to have two famous veterinarians as parents.

3

Together they worked strange cases and were called upon to solve animal-related mysteries all around the world. And sure, it was fabulous to go with them during school breaks to exotic locations and on exciting adventures. But why was everything so far away, and why had no one invented teleportation for real?

"So, how long until we're in Austria?" Lilly sighed and settled in for the long haul.

CHAPTER 2

About twelve hours later, the Cook siblings were sitting in a taxi headed to their new home for the next week.

"You're right in the center of Europe now," explained their friendly driver. "Vienna is our capital, and most of the people speak German in our country. But you are lucky, because we are taught English in school, and you'll be able to talk to children your age as well," he said.

"That will be helpful!" whispered Celia to Lilly and Fynn.

While their parents took care of their animal patients, the three Cook children liked to help uncover some mysteries themselves.

"Look, I bet there are still kings and queens living here!" Fynn pointed out the window.

It really seemed like they had not only crossed the Atlantic Ocean to Europe but also traveled back in time. Cobblestone streets with majestic, tall stone houses on each side, narrow alleys with iron gates leading to hidden courtyards, and even some horse-drawn carriages parked next to medieval looking fountains.

"Well, our last emperor reigned one hundred years ago, until 1918 to be exact. We're proud of our culture here in Austria. Did you know that the famous composer and musician Wolfgang Amadeus Mozart was born in this country? And he was around your age when he performed his own music in front of the empress!" said their Viennese guide.

Celia smiled. Back home, she had just started to practice a new ballet dance to the magical music of Mozart and was thrilled to be in a city filled with such a glorious past. She hoped to find some special moves to include in her routine at home.

"We've almost arrived at your destination," explained the driver, "however, traffic in this part of the old town has become so crazy, it might take us a couple more minutes to drive the final distance to the gate."

Fynn pressed his freckled nose to the car window to see and hear busy cars driving bumper to bumper mixed with some angry honking, all in between the glorious old buildings of Vienna.

Somehow, the picture didn't look right to him. He imagined that only horse-drawn carriages and elegantly dressed people were walking down the narrow streets of the city again, just like in Mozart's times.

CHAPTER 3

"Welcome, welcome, Mr. and Mrs. Cook! Welcome to the world-famous Spanish Riding School in Vienna, children!"

A stout looking man with hair as black as coal and an impressive royal mustache that curled up on both ends opened the back gate for them.

Fynn and Celia couldn't take their eyes off his huge facial decoration, the likes of which they had only seen as photo props for birthday parties so far.

Suddenly, they were standing in a magnificent square courtyard that was cornered by open stables on two sides and what looked like the back windows of a historic palace on the other two sides.

"Who would have thought that this was behind a simple green gate? And why are we at a Spanish school in Austria? Are those not different countries?" wondered Fynn, who could barely contain his excitement, paired with some confusion.

"Guten Tag, Herr Fuchs! I am afraid

saying 'Hello' is the extent of my German vocabulary for now," said Mr. Cook to their host.

"Wunderbar!" laughed Mr. Fuchs, and he walked with the Cook family further into the courtyard. "We have set up the guest quarters for you and your family on the first floor. Some of my Eleves will get your suitcases."

"Elves?" Celia couldn't help but cry out. "There are real elves at your palace?"

Now all three adults started giggling, and poor Celia blushed until even the tips of her ears burned red.

Mr. Fuchs tussled her brown bob

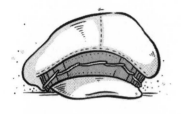 and explained, "The Eleves are our cadets who learn proper horse care, cleaning, and riding with the goal of becoming a fully qualified Rider one day. But you know what, our cadets are rather like little elves around here. I might just start calling them that from now on!"

Celia smiled at their host with his twinkling eyes. She could have sworn that even the ends of his complicated mustache were winking at her.

"I really think it's time for a tour and history lesson of this place," said her mom as she took the twins by the hand and motioned for Lilly to follow them.

CHAPTER 4.

Together the Cook family walked into the first stable building, and the noble heads of a dozen nosy horses peeking over their stable bars immediately surrounded them. Their beautiful, long mane fell around large, black eyes that looked at the visitors curiously. Gentle neighs and the sound of shuffling hooves filled the barn around them.

Mr. Cook approached the first stall and gently touched one of the stallions. He began to tell the story of the Spanish Riding School and its famous snow white dancing horses, the Lipizzaner.

"Kids, you're standing in the oldest riding school in the world. The 'Spanish' part of the name, Fynn, originates from the horses. They came from the country of Spain and were especially spirited and thought to be good for the special art performed here, the High School for horses."

"Which probably has nothing to do with high school for students back home?" added Lilly.

Her dad shook his head. "No, the *'Haute École'* or 'High School' in horse language are very advanced forms of dressage based on the horses' natural movements, almost like a horse ballet. Today's Lipizzaner stallions are the proud children of the Spanish breed with Italian and Arab bloodlines, and they are specially bred and trained all their lives to master the art of dancing in these classical performances."

"Like members of the New York City Ballet back home?" asked Celia.

"Yes, sweetie, just like a classical ballet dancer. In fact, these horses have dance moves that sound very similar to the ones you study in class: the *piaffe,* the *passage,* and *pirouettes,* too!" chimed in her mom.

Suddenly, a sad little voice joined their conversation from one of the stables, "Unfortunately, you won't be able to see them perform now. It would be so much better to show you a *piaffe,* where they trot in place, or even a *levade,* standing only on their hind hooves. But now, 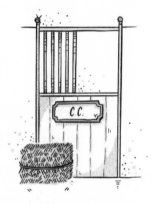 we can't show you anything because none of them dance..." and with that, the voice got cut off by the sound of tears and sniffing.

·CHAPTER 5·

"I see you've met my son, Max!" said Mr. Fuchs joining them in the stable building at that moment. "And I guess, he has presented our little problem for you. It has been two months and three days since our world-famous stallions stopped dancing. We have had their regular veterinarians and experts here day and night, but since everyone and everything has failed, we're placing our last hope in

your experience with mysterious cases all around the world."

At this, Max stepped out of the stable, patted a last goodbye to a beautiful, gleaming white stallion, and pulled the door with the golden name tag "Conversano Calcedona" shut behind him.

Standing in front of the Cook kids was a slim, dark-haired boy about Lilly's age with huge dark eyes that were glistening wet. Wiping his nose with the back of his hand, he looked at them skeptically.

"Well, I hope you don't want to try any magic potions on them," he said. "We have certainly had our share of that, and let me tell you, Calce does not appreciate dried frog legs or pulverized spiderwebs mixed into his food."

Fynn laughed out loud and took a step closer to Max and "Calce's" door. "Well, I hope the two of you aren't angry if my mom chants some magic words in here at midnight, then?"

Max stared at him for a moment with his mouth open before finally offering a grin and an approving nod. It was one of the twin's special talents to win over even the most skeptical stranger.

"Come on, I'll show you around!" Max exclaimed.

"That's an excellent idea, son. The four of you can explore the stables and the courtyard a little more while the doctors and I discuss some details and look at the charts in my office. I'm sure, you have lots of questions for me," added Mr. Fuchs walking outside with Mr. and Mrs. Cook.

CHAPTER 6

"Have you spent all your life with these horses? Do you have a favorite? Do you ever get to ride them?" Lilly started hammering Max with questions the second their parents left.

Max continued strolling down the corridor and passed a pat here and there to the royal muzzles appearing on both sides. "Yes. Yes. And not yet..." he offered while walking ahead.

"As most of the Eleves here, my father began his career at sixteen and has spent his entire life living and working with these special horses. It takes around eight to twelve years to become a fully qualified Rider, years in which many give up, and only the very best succeed. And then you still must work hard to become the Chief Rider or even the First Chief Rider. My father has spent over 35 years mastering his craft."

"Wow!" exclaimed all three Cook kids at the same time. They could hardly picture any other job where you would be in training for such a long time.

"Here I thought our parents had a long and tough education when they decided to become veterinarians," added Lilly.

"You really live and breathe horses when you decide to become part of the Spanish Riding School," said Max. "In the beginning, you don't even have to know your way around horses or how to ride. You start by learning proper horse care as well as handling of all the equipment, like cleaning saddles and bridles. You also get regular riding lessons  on a fully trained School Stallion, but for the first years only on the lunge, which is basically a long leash that one of the Chief Riders controls. There are daily school lessons about the history and long-standing traditions of the school and of classical horsemanship."

While he was talking, the kids had crossed the courtyard and reached a separate building, which they now entered. Here, the feeling was different, as they heard loud neighing, impatient scraping and bumping.

Celia stretched on her ballerina tiptoes to get a good look inside one of the boxes. "Hey, these horses are either really dusty, or they are not real Lipizzaner at all!" she wondered.

The three kids crowded around one of the roomy stalls where a gorgeous gray and white freckled neck arched high and began sweeping up and down in excitement.

CHAPTER 7

"Meet Pluto Alea! Pluto, these are our visitors from America," introduced Max. "Pluto is a four-year-old stallion who is one of our rising stars. He mastered all the skills to advance to the Spanish Riding School and will soon be assigned to an Assistant Rider. Together they will train for the next six years until they can both successfully participate in the Spanish Riding School Quadrille for the first time."

"But why isn't he snow white like the other horses?" asked Celia.

"Well, look around the young stallions' stable, and tell me what you see!" said Max.

The words were hardly spoken when Fynn started running back and forth, shouting, "Gray!" and "Gray again!" and "Little white but mostly gray!"

Max laughed. "Exactly! This is one of the amazing facts. Lipizzaner are born dark, usually bay or black, and they become lighter each year, turning gray and speckled gray and white. After about six or ten years, their transformation is complete, and they're all white.

"It's kind of like your hair that's turning darker the older you get. Only the other way 'round," teased Celia turning to Lilly. Her sister who had been fair blond in all their baby pictures, now only had a couple of blond strands left in her shoulder-length hair.

"That's truly amazing!" said Lilly, who was already in love with these Austrian horses. Or were they really Spanish? She still couldn't wrap her head around all the facts and history that she had just learned in this short amount of time.

Suddenly, her head really spun, and she yawned. She felt the time difference catching up with her. Was it evening here or at home? Had they really just arrived in this magical land of horses and riding this morning? And what about her parents? Were they any closer to solving the mystery of the dancing horses that didn't want to dance?

"I think I'm ready to crash!" admitted Fynn, and he tugged on Max's sleeve. "Can you show us where they brought my suitcase? I have this amazing monster truck video that we can watch on my tablet."

"And I need to ask your opinion about my Mozart ballet recital music, which I brought along," Celia chimed in. "Maybe we can listen to it together, and you'll give me some advice?"

"I do love monster trucks but I have not the faintest idea about Mozart or his music. Sorry, Celia, you are on your own with your dancing!" said Max and took off running towards the guest rooms.

CHAPTER 8

The next morning, the Cook family was sitting at a café just around the corner deciding what food to try for their first Austrian breakfast.

They were cramped around a small round table with a white marble top, sitting on five ancient-looking, wobbly chairs covered with red velvet cloth.

All around them perfectly dressed people were reading  different newspapers stretched onto giant, ancient looking wooden newspaper holders that Celia had never seen before.

Even the breakfast places had a fairytale feel to them, thought Celia when comparing her current location to their favorite diner in her hometown. How on earth do you put the newspaper on these wooden holders each morning? And do they make them in small sizes for reading on your tablet, too?

"I really wonder if the food is going to be as good as at the diner at home."

Her twin pulled her back to reality with his question.

The café menu listed some sweet bakery items filled with jams, some egg dishes, hot chocolate variations, and so many coffee choices that Mr. and Mrs. Cook had a difficult time deciding.

"How can there be 50 combinations of how to prepare your coffee?" wondered Mr. Cook and rubbed his tired eyes. "I really just need to wake up this morning!" Their dad was clearly suffering from jet lag, too.

"How was your first meeting with Mr. Fuchs and the horses yesterday, Dad?" asked Lilly.

"Well, that's just it, sweetie. I simply can't wrap my head around the problem and its cause yet," admitted her dad. "Your mom and I were up into the wee hours trying to sort through the notes and gather our thoughts. There is nothing physically wrong with any of these horses. No virus, no bacteria, nothing."

Celia creased her eyebrows deep in thought. "It would almost have to be something contagious if all of the dancing horses are suffering from it..."

Her mom nodded. Their parents had always encouraged them to take part in case discussions and to offer their thoughts and opinions. Their dad said that kids could lend a different perspective to everything since their heads were much closer to the earth. Lilly and the twins agreed with that! Although some days Lilly felt that her head was rather stuck in the clouds, which would give her an even better view.

"What would you kids like to do this morning?" Mrs. Cook interrupted her train — or rather plane — of thought. "I can take you around the city a little bit before I have to join your dad back at the stables for the exams."

"Mom, can we see the armory, where they kept their weapons in ancient times?" shouted Fynn excitedly.

"You're so predictable, Fifi!" scolded

Celia, using his special nickname to annoy him. Sometimes she wondered how they could even be related.

"I'd like to visit the Mozart House so I can learn some more about him for my ballet class back home," she continued.

Fynn stuck out his tongue and rolled his eyes. "Look which annoying twin was talking about being predictable, Miss Tutu!" he said and wondered how on earth they could be related to each other.

Mrs. Cook had to laugh at her combination of twins, and she answered peacefully, "How about we eat our breakfast now and take a stroll around the neighborhood after we've filled our tummies? I'm sure Vienna will offer something for each one of us!"

CHAPTER 9

When the satisfied family left the café, Mr. Cook turned left to make his way back to his consult with the horses while the rest of the family strolled to their right down a narrow alley, paved with cobblestones and flanked by cute little shops.

Fynn was drawn to a shop window filled with antique silver items, ranging from the usual mirrors and frames to the most amazing tiny figurines, and yes, polished silver knives and daggers, glittering in the light.

Lilly stood next door at a shop selling hand-carved and painted wooden cuckoo clocks and other decorative items. Celia had dragged her mother to the other side of the street, pointing at several unique Austrian shirts in bold patterns and colors.

They continued their journey down the streets, turning left and right, admiring each unique house and special monument. All the buildings were

so different from what they had seen before.

"Everything is so old and seems like it has a history of its own." Celia admired the house they were just passing.

"You're right, Celia! I bet each one could tell a story about its long life and all the interesting characters that have lived in it so far," said her mom.

They passed the Column of the Plague, which was sculpted in the seventeenth century to remember the victims of the Black Death. This illness of the bubonic plague had wiped out a third of the people throughout the continent of Europe.

When Fynn asked, they took a detour, first climbing 343 steps atop Vienna's most famous landmark, the tower of St. Stephen's Cathedral and then exploring deep down under the church to see the ancient catacombs. These were tombs with bones stacked high in underground caves, enough to make even Fynn's skin crawl with creepiness.

The kids were glad to step outside and into the breathtaking beauty and calm of the church square again. Celia looked around and pointed at a green sign, "Look, Mom! There's a sign to the Mozart House! Can we please take a quick tour?"

With the promise of taking a break for some famous Austrian cake and hot cocoa after this very last stop, her siblings agreed to come along as well.

"Bribe me with food, and I'll follow you everywhere, Celia!" joked her twin brother.

"Even back into the catacombs?" said Celia.

Lilly moaned impatiently. She just wanted to get back to the horses and Max! After all, that was what they were here for. Although, she had to admit how important it was to learn something about the environment and background of the patients as well. A tricky case could never be solved by itself. One always had to think of all the surrounding factors.

She had picked up this idea while watching her parents with some of their more puzzling cases around the world. Like the time they had been called to New York City to investigate the rowdy packs of dogs in Central Park. She still remembered their long walks through the park to take in all the factors.

But that was a story for another time, thought Lilly, pulling herself back to her current case in Vienna and following her family to the house of the famous composer, Wolfgang Amadeus Mozart.

"CHAPTER 10."

Stepping through the door of the simple but prettily decorated house where Mozart spent some of his last years, Celia took a deep breath. Her skin prickled with the faint sound of the grand music that was written here.

"No wonder he composed more music during his years here than anywhere else," she said, "with St. Stephen's

Cathedral around the corner and all these treasures inspiring you."

"Yes, it felt like I could write my very own masterpiece as soon as we entered!" scoffed Fynn at his twin. Celia narrowed her eyes and sighed. Why did her brother have to mock her passions all the time? Shaking her head she pushed ahead into the building.

The family climbed to the third floor, where Mozart and his wife Constanze and their two sons had lived in one of the most elegant apartments with four large connecting rooms, two small ones, plus a roomy kitchen. The rooms were decorated with antique furniture and showed interesting trinkets from Mozart's era. Lilly and Fynn crowded around a display with an old cuckoo clock, watching how its ancient gears were still ticking and moving.

In the meantime, Celia had continued walking through the apartment, reading the information boards on the walls: Mozart lived in this house from 1784 to 1787. He played the piano and violin before age five and was considered a child genius. In one picture Mozart was performing for funnily dressed royalty when he was only a little boy. He composed more than 600 pieces of music.

"And, here he is sitting in the courtyard of the Spanish Riding School," she mumbled to herself.

Wait a minute... Celia called for her siblings to come over. They crowded in front of the painting. The children recognized the courtyard they had just left this morning and the stables with the majestic Lipizzaner curiously watching as Mozart sat and busily scribbled something on large pieces of paper.

"This is amazing!" exclaimed their mom who had come over to see what her children were looking at. "And it also reminds me that we have to make our way back to the riding school. I promised your dad I'd be there for his afternoon visit with the horses. Let's see if he has made any progress this morning."

Yes, hopefully, there would be some news waiting for them, wished Lilly. After all, they had told Max that their parents would make his dancing horses perform again.

CHAPTER 11

Cake and hot chocolate were all forgotten as the Cook children and their mom raced back through Vienna's old town.

They could already see the gates to the Spanish Riding School when Celia slowed down suddenly. Heavenly music was floating out of the large doors of the church next door.

She only had time to glance at the large poster board "Mozart's *Requiem* Concert tonight, 18:00, Michaeler Church" and remembered to ask  her parents if she could walk over to listen to the concert later. If only she knew what time 18:00 was. Why did things in Europe have to be so different from back home? Even a simple thing such as telling the time seemed to be lost in translation.

She raced after her family toward the big green gates and came to a full stop before crossing the small alley. Two cars were screeching their tires and honking at her as they speeded by.

"Oh, how I wish there were no more cars in this town!" said Celia angrily. Out of breath and flustered, she met up with the rest of her family crowded around her dad in the courtyard just in time to see his disappointed face and slumped shoulders.

"Where were you, slowpoke? Dad has no clue what's going on with the horses," whispered Fynn.

Apparently, they had ruled out all known illnesses after performing test after test and consulting the notes that hordes of other experts had left regarding the non-dancing horses.

"I think the next step is to see the horses in action," said Dr. Cook.

Or rather inaction, thought Lilly but kept her mouth shut. As an animal lover herself, she knew how much her parents fretted over every patient in their care. She remembered how sad she had felt when her pet chickens wouldn't eat for a couple of days, and she spent every waking minute by their coop to find out what was going on.

Since animals couldn't talk, they left humans feeling helpless when serious problems arose. Then she also remembered that all her hours of observation had led her to solve her own mystery chicken case.

A giant hawk had taken up post in one of the tall trees around the coop and was sitting motionless hour after hour watching her poor chickens.

Lilly, with her human eyes, had not detected the camouflaged bird, but the chickens were so stressed about the constant presence of the feared predator that they simply stopped eating. A simple plastic owl decoy hung by the chicken coop solved the problem, and the hawk soon moved on to find easier prey. Her pet chickens had been happy ever since.

So Lilly couldn't wait to get a chance to observe the dancing horses and maybe draw her very own conclusions in this mysterious case.

CHAPTER 12

"Hey guys, are you ready to watch your very first performance of the world-famous Lipizzan horses?" asked Max, joining them in the courtyard, giving them a hopeful smile.

Fynn turned to his new friend and was shocked by how terrible Max looked this morning. Someone did not have a good night's sleep around here!

Fynn had a great idea. He shouted to his buddy "Last one in his seat is a rotten egg!" and took off in a sprint with Max shouting in German and trailing his heels. Fynn always knew exactly what his audience wanted.

They entered a large arena that was decorated more like a ballroom with gold ornaments on the walls and chandeliers hanging over the riding ring. Royal chairs covered in red velvet placed on beautiful balconies instead of plain bleachers framed the arena.

"They sure do like their red velvet around here," laughed Celia.

It did look more like an opera house than a riding arena for certain. No wonder the horses danced in here.

As soon as the Cook family and Max took their seats spread out on the balcony, glorious music came through the hidden speakers, and the chandelier lights began to twinkle and glimmer.

Lilly felt a shudder of sweet anticipation take hold: how lucky she was to experience her own private performance of the world-famous dancing horses today!

However, her excitement turned out to be in vain. After eight beautifully dressed riders rode eight white stallions in a well-organized single file into the room, the performance started falling apart. Horses were running left and right, suddenly stopping in the deep sand of the arena and running in crazy circles. The whole show looked more like eight circus clowns performing with their trained horses to entertain laughs from the audience.

"This is horrible!" exclaimed Celia, full of empathy for the riders and their majestic creatures. She could only imagine how it felt to fail so miserably at a performance, even if it was in front of a private audience. "It's like I would stumble and fall over my own feet when dancing," she whispered.

"Or performing a hip-hop routine to your darling Mozart's music," added Fynn.

"You have to give credit to these riders though," said their older sister. "I'm sure I'd have to hang on for dear life if my horse behaved in such a strange way. You can really tell that they have been trained for years and years and understand their horses' moves even before they complete them."

Unfortunately, despite all their horse sense, they still couldn't bring their beloved horses to perform in the way they had been trained to. And this became dreadfully clear to the entire small audience right away.

CHAPTER 13

The Lipizzaner left the arena with both riders' and horses' heads hung low and were followed by Mr. Fuchs leading a breathtaking stallion into the ring.

"Calce!" breathed Max in their direction.

Fynn noticed the small boy's hands were cramped in hope, and his brow furrowed. It looked like he was willing his favorite horse to give his best for the visitors today.

"My dad will perform the *Haute École,* remember, the High School, with Calce. Here he leads him on the long reins, standing behind and next to the horse while giving him small commands to perform the poses they've practiced all these years."

The Cook children and their parents held their breaths as the impressive stallion seemed to gather his gaits, compress his sleek white body, and catapult himself into the air. His four massive hooves left the sandy ground of the arena and hovered in midair for a moment, before stomping onto the earth in the exact same spot they had taken off only a few milliseconds ago.

There were no graceful kicks in the air, no *levades* or even beautiful *caprioles,* all poses the children had only read about and seen in the paintings and photographs around the riding school but had yet to witness with their own eyes.

The head of the Spanish Riding School continued to ask his horse to perform, begging him with subtle encouragements around the arena. Nothing much happened, and it became very painful to watch the efforts of this impressive and usually successful team.

Finally, a tired and red-faced Mr. Fuchs tipped his hat toward Mr. and Mrs. Cook and the kids and led Calce out of the arena. Celia could have sworn that the ends of his lovely mustache drooped to the ground as he marched outside.

"Max!" she heard her brother shout.

Their Austrian friend had just jumped up with an almost silent scream and stormed out of the arena pushing the red velvet chairs left and right along his way.

"We have to follow him!" Fynn rushed after the boy. All he wanted to do was to find and comfort his new friend in this sad moment.

His sisters jumped up as well, and all three kids raced outside, leaving their parents sitting in their chairs deep in thought. The veterinarians were as disappointed by the lack in performance as their kids and had a lot on their minds to discuss.

"Max, stop!" shouted Fynn running across the courtyard. "Wait for us! Wait!"

The little boy showed no signs of stopping or even slowing down and continued his desperate run with the Cook kids on his tail.

They passed a group of Eleves walking the horses in circles for their cooldown, another group of barn helpers

cleaning the stables, always close behind
Max but never quite catching up with him.

They flew past the barn of the young
stallions. Their curious heads followed
the wild chase, and their small hooves
excitedly stomped against the stable doors.

They saw Max enter what seemed to
be a narrow door leading to a tack room.
He wound his way through the gleaming
bridles and saddles that hung in neat rows
on both walls.

"Max, where are you going?" Lilly began to worry now. She didn't remember seeing this part of the Spanish Riding School on their official tour the day before. Where was the frantic boy taking them today? Were they allowed to be back here or would they get into trouble?

CHAPTER 14

When the Cook siblings finally stopped and gathered their breaths to look around, it took them a moment to realize where they were.

Through the long and narrow tack room, they had entered a dusty, even older looking barn with only four large stalls that were decorated with grand looking nameplates and golden inscriptions. There were beautiful saddles and gorgeous bridles hung next to each door, their metal bits gleaming a rich yellow like they were made of real gold. Where had Max brought them? And where was he?

"Max?" called Lilly carefully, her voice almost dropping to a whisper in this strange room.

"What is this stable? Where are we?" Fynn said. "I'm so sorry about how the performance went today. Please have faith in our parents, Max. They'll give their best to help your horses, I promise!"

Max stepped out of a shady corner. "I can't help it, Fynn! You've to understand that this riding school is all I've known. I'm scared about what will happen to the horses and us if they don't start to dance again. What will people think of my father? I don't want him to be the last head of the Spanish Riding School who couldn't get his horses to dance after almost 300 years of performances."

Celia and Lilly stepped up to the boy and hugged him tightly from both sides. They stayed huddled for several minutes, feeling how his breathing steadied until he finally let out a big exhale. You could almost feel the negative thoughts pouring out of Max's body with one deep breath. "Sometimes a silent embrace offers everything you need to say in that moment," thought Celia to herself.

"So guys, this is the oldest part of the Riding School. The four horses here are some of the most prized fathers and mothers of our horses dating back to the eight original stallions that created the breed. They're officially retired and are only shown for special celebrations with their beautiful tack, which you can see next to their barn doors. I'm really not supposed to bring anyone back here because Pluto, Conversano, Maestoso, and Neapolitano are really old and don't like visitors anymore," admitted Max.

Fynn bravely took a step forward toward the barn doors. The air was musky, and he still couldn't glimpse even the faintest shape of these majestic Lipizzaner in their roomy stalls.

"These are original horses of the Lipizzan bloodline!" exclaimed Lilly in awe. Oh, how she wished Max would let them stay here and see

or even touch one of these magical creatures. As she pictured a grand stallion leaping into the air, wearing his beautiful saddle and gleaming bridle, she traced her fingers over the dark leather hanging on one of the doors.

"What on earth did this boy think bursting into here, dragging these unannounced visitors behind him? And how many are there anyway, they smell all the same to me..." Lilly suddenly heard

a creaky voice sounding from the back
corner of the stall with the "Pluto Austria"
nameplate shining on its door.

CHAPTER 15

"Hello? Who just said that?" Lilly looked up in panic, dropping the reins she had held between her fingers. Had someone followed them back here? Would they get in trouble because they were not supposed to be in here?

She really didn't want their parents to find out. They would get angry and maybe stop taking them around the world to help animals in need. The other kids had heard her shout out and gathered around looking concerned.

"Lilly, what happened?" they all whispered.

"Shhh! Someone's in here with us," she answered, putting her index finger to her mouth. Everyone froze and concentrated on the dark room.

"This is not funny, Lilly!" Celia scolded after a silent minute.

"You scared us! Max said we were not supposed to be back here." Celia expected this kind of joke from their brother but not from her "oh, I am so grown-up" big sister.

Lilly couldn't hear anything either and frowned in frustration. She reached out to stroke the warm leather of the reins one more time.

"I wish they would leave now," she heard the same voice exclaim again.

"Seriously now, Pluto! Finally something happens around here, and all you do is nag, nag, nag, nag!" responded a second, warm and motherly voice this time.

"Aaarghh!" shouted Lilly, and she jumped in fear. What was going on in this place? Where were all the voices coming from?

"Lilly!" she heard Max's stern voice. "Stop screeching, or we will have to leave this instant. I told you these horses are not used to excitement anymore."

"Oh, how I wish we'd have some more excitement around here!" the second voice said.

"I miss the music above all," replied a third, deep and booming voice as well.

"Guys, I don't know what is going on." Lilly trembled. "But I think these horses are talking to each other!"

Her siblings and new friend couldn't believe their ears. What had she just said? Now Celia was worried. Maybe the jet lag or something even worse was catching up with her sister.

"Seriously, I swear! I can hear three voices having a conversation!" repeated Lilly.

They all stepped up to the doors and glanced over the gate into the stall of the horse named Pluto Austria. A gorgeous white mare with a brocade blanket over her white flanks looked at them with a distinct air of mistrust, which made both Max and Fynn flinch back and grab the reins hung by the door to steady themselves.

"Eeeew, there are so many of them! And now they are spreading their dangerous children germs right into my room. Shoo, shoo!" the boys heard an angry voice declare.

"Celia, you have to listen to this!" urged Fynn while grabbing Celia's hand.

"There, there... Calm down, Pluto darling! There isn't anything we haven't seen throughout all our long years, have we?" boomed the calm voice from across the barn coming from the door with the "Maestoso Musica" signage.

What a beautiful name, thought Celia before fully understanding what she had just witnessed. Lilly had been right; these horses were all talking to each other!

CHAPTER 16

"Oh, I remember well," continued the mare with the "Conversano Capriola" nameplate, stepping up to the divider of her stall. "Wasn't it just twenty-something years ago that we were almost lost in that big fire? I can still smell the scent of ashes in my nostrils. Brrrr..."

The Cook kids didn't dare open their mouths but looked at Max with wide eyes.

He leaned in to whisper, "On a night about twenty years ago, a fire started in one of the historic buildings, but all our horses were thankfully saved. The pictures of people leading these precious horses out of the flames and tying them up outside in the squares were in all the papers and on TV back then."

The Lipizzaner didn't seem to take note of any of their conversations and continued to talk about their memories instead.

"How about the time when they took us aboard that large vehicle on the water, and we traveled forever and ever." Lilly recognized the complaining, nasal voice of Pluto talking now.

"Yes, I remember!" exclaimed Maestoso. "When we finally were led out of the boat, so many humans came to greet us, and music boomed all around us, coming from different, shiny objects that they carried around."

"Was that the time when the guy they called President Reagan rode on my back, holding the reins in one hand and wearing a silly hat?" wondered Conversano.

"I thought he was an actor," mused Pluto.

Fynn beamed; just yesterday upon their arrival he had seen the framed picture of US President Ronald Reagan sitting on a majestic white Lipizzaner in one of the

hallways leading to their chambers at the riding School.

Now he knew that the beautiful mare in the picture was Conversano. She still remembered this famous encounter, even though the president had apparently attempted to ride in a Western cowboy style. These horses had awesome powers! Not only were they talking to each other, but they were also remembering events that had taken place a lifetime ago.

"How about that dreadful day when those first two girl humans started meddling around the stables here?" the unhappy voice of Pluto chirped up again. "That was a disaster waiting to happen!"

Max couldn't help but burst out with a loud guffaw, and all the kids immediately dropped the magic reins and looked at him questioningly.

"I think she's referring to the day in 2008, when after a long battle, the first female Eleves started their training with the Spanish Riding School in Vienna for the very first time in its existence. Before that, only boys could become part of the team here."

Well, that was just about time, thought Celia to herself. She would have expected a little more support from a mare though!

Taking advantage of their break in listening to the horse conversations, Lilly stepped over to the last barn door and wondered, "Why is this one not talking?"

They all huddled up in front of the nameplate "Neapolitano Aquileja" — which was quite a mouthful to read — and stretched on their toes to look over the bars.

In the farthest corner, another majestic stallion covered in an ornate blanket was standing motionless with his head hung low. His whole posture was screaming despair to the kids, and Max let out another deep, frustrated sigh.

"It seems that he has caught whatever has affected our performing horses as well," he stated sadly. "Let's go back to the main court."

Excited neighing accompanied their exit, and even without the power of the magic reins, Lilly could have sworn that she heard Pluto's distinct voice calling after them, "Good riddance, smelly creatures!"

CHAPTER 17

The children decided to treat themselves to some long overdue Austrian chocolate cake and hot chocolate and digest what they had just overheard at the old stables.

They checked in with their parents who were still busy talking about various charts, then exited the grand, hunter-green gates of the riding school. The kids crossed the busy cobblestone road over to the coffee shop where they had enjoyed breakfast just this morning. "Back when we had not the faintest idea that horses would talk!" thought Lilly.

The mood lifted as soon as they dug into their pieces of rich chocolate cake, layered with apricot jam and with a generous dollop of fresh whipped cream.

"This is fabulous, just what the doctors ordered!" exclaimed Fynn.

"Funny story," explained Max, "this chocolate cake, the *Sacher Torte*, is easily the best known Austrian dessert around the world. It was created in the 1800s by a

sixteen-year-old kitchen boy for a prince, when the master baker got sick."

"Who says that kids can't run the world!" claimed Lilly with her mouth full of gooey yumminess.

"Exactly! And that is why we have to solve the case of the horses who won't dance. It doesn't seem that our parents are getting any closer to finding the truth," said Celia to her siblings and friend.

Since they had listened in on the horses' voices an hour ago, it was crystal clear that the solution was in their able eight-year-old and ten-year-old hands.

"So, how about your speaking horses,

Max?" Fynn asked. He was still surprised by all those distinct voices and humanlike conversations they had overheard.

Max shook his head in disbelief. In all his years as the son of the head riding master, he had never experienced anything like this. If anyone had told him this morning that horses talked to each other or even that horses remembered things from the past as humans did, he would have called an ambulance. And even the Cook kids, children of famous veterinarians, who had been around all species of animals all their lives, had never believed this to be possible.

"Well, since we can't possibly be all having the same dream, we have to accept the fact that these horses can talk and that the reins somehow act as a portal for us to understand what they are saying," explained Lilly matter-of-factly. "I'd suggest, we use this chance to help us investigate the case of the Lipizzaner. I wonder if they can tell us what is wrong with their dancing friends."

Fynn scratched his head. He wasn't sure how they could steer the conversation to that topic. It wasn't like the horses had heard them or even reacted to their voices. In fact, they had seemed rather disturbed by their smelly presence in their well-hidden barn. They couldn't just prance in and ask them questions, could they?

Celia shoved the last piece of chocolate

cake into her mouth, washed it down with the rich hot chocolate, and exclaimed, "We'll have to continue this conversation later. I have to get back and get ready for my concert at the church tonight. Mom promised to take me over."

CHAPTER 18

Celia could hardly contain her excitement as she made her way to the church next door hand in hand with her mother.

They had both taken a quick shower and changed into something more elegant for the concert. Mrs. Cook was wearing a long black skirt and blouse with a colorful scarf wrapped around her broad shoulders. Celia was thrilled to be dressed in her favorite special-occasion dress, which she had brought along to Austria just in case. The pale pink layers of tulle twirled and spun as she danced and hopped around her mom along their short walk.

At the entrance, they received a small flyer describing tonight's performance.

"Mom," whispered Celia urgently. "They are really performing Mozart's *Requiem* tonight!" Celia knew from her ballet classes and yesterday's short visit to the Mozart House here in Vienna that Mozart wrote the *Requiem*, his very last piece, while he lived in this city. Maybe even while he was sitting in the courtyard of the Riding School, just as they had seen in the painting at the museum.

Sadly, this was a special piece of music which he had never finished before he passed away. The flyer explained that ever since his death on December 5, 1791, Mozart's *Requiem* was performed almost weekly at the church.

"That means they have been playing his music here for more than 225 years," said Celia.

"Almost as long as the Spanish Riding School has been next door," replied her mother. "Didn't it first open its doors to the horses around 1735?"

Music and dancing horses... Celia could almost grasp an important connection in the back of her mind. The thought slipped away as quickly as it had entered, and the enormous organ pipes began their first festive sounds.

Soon the entire church was filled with the deep, soulful tones of Wolfgang Amadeus Mozart's last masterpiece. Celia and her mom lost themselves in the music of another era and left worries about horses who would not dance far behind them for a while.

"Oh, Mom, I'm so inspired for my ballet recital back home.

I want to project the feeling of the cold, damp church and the sounds of the organ booming throughout my body. The music actually warmed my body if you would believe it!" Celia beamed. "And then, I want to..."

"Watch out!" screamed Mrs. Cook, and she pulled her daughter back from the curb at the very last minute. "My goodness, these cars really need to take it slow. They almost came up on the curb, driving around that narrow corner. And you, young lady, need to keep your dreamy eyes open when walking around these city streets."

Celia's face turned pale; this had been a close call with the car almost brushing the tips of her dancing toes. How could this enchanted old part of the city, with the church just across the cobblestone street from the riding School have such a bad traffic problem?

Again, she wished all the noisy cars away, replaced by horse-drawn carriages and elegantly dressed families strolling around, listening to the faint sounds of Mozart's music, which carried through the streets from the Michaeler Church.

CHAPTER 19

The Cook family was invited to dinner at the apartment of Max and his parents, located in the main part of the riding School, across the courtyard from their beautiful guest quarters.

In true Austrian fashion, the apartment had tall ceilings, original antique wooden floors, and was furnished with many interesting horse-inspired knick-knacks. After a short tour, the guests settled into their seats to sample their very first taste of true Austrian home cooking, courtesy of Max's mom. She brought a clear chicken soup with soft dumplings, followed by fried cutlets with a delicious side of potato salad.

The table with the four adults was exchanging the usual pleasantries about the apartment, the meal, and the kindness of the hosts. The kids' table was unusually quiet and whispering frantically. Celia learned that the three other children had not found any new clues while she had attended the concert at the church. On the contrary, Lilly and the boys had fallen into a chocolate cake induced food coma, and they rested with their books and video games, waiting for her to come back.

"I had the best evening! You guys should have come with me instead of being lazy," gushed Celia.

She continued telling them about the music flowing through the church and all the interesting facts she had picked up from the flyer at the concert.

"I had no idea that the church has been playing Mozart's pieces for as long as our horses have been around!" said Max. It seemed that this aspect of his native Austrian traditions had not been known to him at all.

Lilly and Fynn were both chewing their lips, focusing on some similar, distant thoughts that they couldn't quite identify. "Mozart, music, dancing horses..." mumbled Lilly.

She was interrupted by Celia's animated account of how she almost lost her ballerina toes because of two honking cars speeding around the corner next to the riding school.

"I'm so glad you are ok!" exclaimed Fynn.

Although his twin sister was the most annoying person he knew – well, honestly right up there with his older sister – he always looked out for her. And those pesky

cars driving so close to the precious horses had been bothering him all along.

After the meal, the parents gathered the children together in the living room. Their faces were sad and serious, and when Mrs. Cook pulled her twins into an embrace, Fynn knew that the news wouldn't be good.

"I'm so sorry," began Mr. Fuchs, "but we wanted to tell you before we make it public in the morning. After talking with the doctors, I've decided to close the Spanish Riding School until further notice. We'll be sending the horses back to the farm where they are born and hope that a vacation away from the city might work the miracle that none of us could.

The Spanish Riding School will take its first break after 283 years," he concluded with tears in his eyes, and the ends of his mustache drooped low and listless.

CHAPTER 20.

"No, no, no, no... this can't be happening. I need some air!" exclaimed Max, and he dragged the three siblings outside with him down two flights of stairs and out into the courtyard.

The sun had set, and the warm lights of old-fashioned lanterns lit the perfect rectangle of the courtyard. Eleves were still scurrying around, putting some finishing

touches on their evening routine of bringing hay to the horses and sweeping the barns for the night.

"Look, Max!" Fynn pointed to a remote corner of the courtyard where four unusual horses with baroque looking quilts on their backs were patiently standing while getting their feet brushed. "Let's get closer to our talking friends."

The children walked up close to the majestic horses. They tried to listen hard, however, without the magic reins, they could not hear anything but the soft neighing and some impatient stomping here and there.

Unfortunately, the hard working Eleves were not impressed by their being there either. One even called out to Max in German, asking him if it wasn't past his bedtime yet.

Max and Fynn angrily put their heads together for a minute, whispered frantically, and then Max called out something in German.

Suddenly, the Eleves put their brushes away and hurried toward the main apartment building.

"What did you boys say?" laughed Lilly.

"Oh, we told them that my father had an important announcement to make to all staff in the office and that they would probably be missing it. I promised we would watch Pluto, Conversano, Maestoso, and Neapolitano for them. I didn't promise anything about not touching them though." Max winked.

"Come on!" he said, gesturing to the children, who huddled around Conversano, whom they remembered as being the friendliest old-timer. They all reached out to touch her leather halter and readied their minds as much as possible before diving into the horse talk.

"...just get over yourself, Pluto!" they heard Conversano exclaiming. "Let's all enjoy this quiet evening outside in our beautiful courtyard. The children are no bother to us at all," the patient mare continued.

The deep, poetic voice of Maestoso chimed in, "Yes, they are not the ones honking and driving those horrible, noisy machines around, are they? Remember when we spent our quiet days out here and listened to the songs that the wind brought us? My father always told me the story of the young lad sitting under the tree and writing music, humming to our ancestors all day long. How can humans create such wonderful magic?"

Lilly's eyes opened wide in amazement: she was certain the horses were talking about Mozart!

Not only did they remember events from their childhoods, or rather foalhoods, they seemed to pass memories down from generation to generation. Oh, how she wished her parents could hear this. Too bad nobody would ever believe her story about the secret minds of horses.

CHAPTER 21

"Luckily, our groomers are coming back to finish my nightly brush."

Lilly was drawn back to the present by the shrill voice of Pluto announcing the return of the Eleves. "Maybe they'll tell these smelly creatures where they belong, once and for all!" the grumpy mare continued.

Alarmed, Lilly and her siblings looked around. Max dropped his hand from the halter first and motioned them to follow him, ducking behind a column and through a small doorway. The children were not in the mood to run into the angry Eleves and answer their questions on their way back from the imaginary meeting that the boys had made up.

"Wow! So how about today's conversation?" exhaled Celia.

"Mozart, music, dancing horses..." mumbled Lilly, just like she had during their dinner conversation earlier.

"What did you just say?" asked Max.

"Oh, just something that has been swirling through my mind all evening: Mozart, music, dancing horses..." answered Lilly.

"And traffic!" exclaimed Fynn. The three Cook children looked at each other in wonder as the puzzle pieces started coming together for them all at once. Could it be? Was this the answer?

A slow smile spread across Celia's face as she said proudly, "Mozart's magic is missing!"

"I'm sorry, but the only one missing something is me!" barked Max. Apparently, their Austrian friend had not followed their mental conversation along.

Lilly, Celia, and Fynn grinned. Their sibling bond reached even beyond the twins. When it came to helping animals, they were in perfect harmony with each other! They were certain that they had just solved the mystery of the dancing horses and could make them perform again.

"Anyone?" demanded Max. His eyes narrowed as he grew very annoyed by being left in the dark.

"Sorry, Max, it just all suddenly started making sense to us," said Celia. "See, when I was at the church concert today, I learned that they had performed Mozart's music almost nightly since the Spanish Riding School opened in this place."

"Then, when we listened to the horses' conversations, we heard how much they enjoy music and how it is almost magic to them," continued Lilly.

"I also remembered Maestoso's comment about the traffic, which made me think of Celia's brush with the crazy honking cars when she crossed the alley between the church and the school," Fynn finished.

Max scratched his freckled nose, and slowly the same grin spread on his face. "You mean, the horses need music, which they can no longer hear over the insane traffic around here?"

"I believe that is exactly what's happening," said Lilly. "Your dancing horses need the magic of music in their stables and in their courtyard to be able to continue dancing."

"And Mozart is not exactly sitting around composing and humming under the tree these days either," laughed Celia.

The children felt excited, their hearts almost bursting with pride and joy. Looking at each other, they all had the same horrible thought though: how on earth could they convince their parents to believe their theory without giving away their secret?

CHAPTER 22

The four expert investigators could barely sleep this short night. They got together in the guest kitchen before the first rays of morning light, long before their parents would awake. Silently munching on pastries left over from the day before, each child was thinking about options and solutions to their problem.

"Well, there is nothing we can do about the terrible traffic right away," said Celia, "so, if the music doesn't reach the dancing horses anymore..."

"...we simply have to bring the music to the horses!" Fynn finished his sister's thoughts out loud.

"Exactly what I was thinking! And I also think, we should end where the trail to the mystery started," announced Max. "Meet me in ten minutes at the entrance to  the old stables! Celia, would you mind bringing your recital music along, too? I think you will need it before your big ballet performance at home after all."

Nine minutes and thirty seconds later the children stormed into the dark, musty stables of the four most royal horses in the Spanish Riding School. They didn't need to touch any magic reins to understand that the tired and irritated neighs and stomps were not a friendly welcome.

The angry stomping grew even more annoyed when Max set-up a small set of wireless speakers and asked Celia to connect her device with the music to it. Soon the dramatic first notes of Mozart's *Requiem* floated through the twilight. Instantly, the horses grew quiet, and the children inched over to the gleaming reins to listen in on their conversations one more time.

"Maestoso, do you hear what I hear?" wondered the gentle voice that Lilly identified as Conversano's.

"How I missed this!" replied the stallion from across the barn.

Suddenly, there was loud rustling, and giant stomps approached the door marked with the sparkling "Neapolitano" sign. A breathtakingly beautiful white head rose above the bars and started swaying to the music. The children held their breaths as their hands connected tightly with the leather reins.

A soft humming sounded from the majestic stallion, and it ebbed and flowed perfectly in tune with Mozart's symphony.

"That horse is singing!" marveled Celia with bright eyes.

"Neapolitano, I thought I would never hear your gorgeous voice again!" purred Pluto in a content manner that was quite different from her behavior so far.

Mozart's magic seemed to touch even the most hard-hearted horse in the stable.

"I would say this treatment is a full success, fellow doctors," declared Lilly happily. "Let's take this show on the road and heal all your dancing horses, Max."

CHAPTER 23.

Mr. Fuchs and the Cook parents could not understand what had happened to their children. Fynn and Max began babbling and urgently dragging them away from the office where they had just started to complete plans to evacuate the precious horses. The adults decided to play along, as everyone understood how hard yesterday's conversation had been for the children.

While walking behind him, Mrs. Cook reached over to smooth Fynn's still sleep-mussed hair. She began to tell him how sometimes one must take a step back from a problem for the sake of the animals.

"Blabber blabber, blah, blah, blah..." was really all that Fynn could hear at that moment. He was already excited about revealing their findings. Why didn't adults ever just wait and listen? Well, that was something his mom would actually tell him to do all the time, so she should maybe just listen to her own advice then. He giggled silently.

When they arrived at the main stables, Max took his position in the middle of the aisle, dramatically raised the speakers above his head, and motioned to Celia to blast Mozart one more time. This time she had chosen the famous song "Queen of the Night" from Mozart's Opera *The Magic Flute*.

"The magic of the flute for some magic from the horses," she said, smiling.

As the powerful voice of the opera singer sounded through the stables, a visible change took place. Formerly sad and fading horses began stepping up to their stall doors, swinging their heads, and even lifting their hooves up and down. The scene in the barn changed drastically. The air of despair and sadness was replaced by upbeat dancing and neighing.

"This is incredible!" exclaimed Mr. Cook.

"Who would have thought?" wondered Mrs. Cook.

"What is the meaning of this all?" asked Mr. Fuchs hopefully.

Now that the children had their parents' full attention, they didn't waste a minute. Taking turns, they explained that they had discovered the effect of music on the horses by accident. They told how they had reasoned that noise levels caused by more and more car traffic in the old part of town around the riding school had disturbed the horses and their sensitive ears.

"These royal horses were accustomed to hearing the sweet sounds of music floating from the church through the courtyard," said Celia.

Lilly thought it best to leave out any details about talking horses and magic reins. Thankfully, the grown-ups were so wrapped up in the answer to their problem that there were no difficult explanations required. Their idea to dazzle them with the hands-on proof had worked its magic!

Handing over the reins to the head of the riding school and the doctors — of course, only figuratively speaking — the children watched in amazement how fast practical solutions to help with the healing process were created. After only a couple of days, modern speaker systems were installed to play soft music in the stables and the courtyard for the horses' benefit. Max and Celia created a playlist and made sure to include plenty of Mozart for the four-legged fans.

CHAPTER 24

On the day of their departure, the entire Cook family, along with their friend Max, gathered in the Spanish Riding School's festive performance hall for the second, and possibly, last time.

Excitement as big as the crystal chandeliers hung in the air. Lilly and her siblings were hopeful that they could finally see the dancing horses in action today.

Nobody wanted a repeat of the disastrous performance from a couple of days ago.

Suddenly, the lights flickered, and gentle notes of classical music filled the room. Celia nervously slid to the rim of her red velvet chair and leaned on the rails to catch her first glimpse of six of her Lipizzaner horse friends galloping into the arena.

From that moment on, there was hardly time to keep up. Majestic horses moved in complicated rows and patterns, always keeping rhythm with their noble riders sitting on their backs and barely moving in their decorated saddles.

Giant hooves stomped the ground, white legs kicked the sand, and flowing tails and manes whirled through the air. Their well-practiced movements had the aura of dancing. Horse and rider became one entity in this magic routine.

The Cook family had barely caught up to everything that was happening down in the arena, when the six riders lined up in the middle and tipped their triangle-shaped hats to them. They gracefully exited the hall, followed by Mr. Fuchs leading his Calce on the lunges.

"He's preparing for the schools above the ground!" whispered Fynn, proudly displaying the phrase he had learned during his short time in Vienna.

He knew the movements in theory, now it was up to Calce and his master leader to show them in real life.

And the horse and his rider didn't disappoint. Calce gathered his strength and performed jumps, kicks, and pirouettes that none of the visitors had considered possible before.

"He seems to be defying gravity!" exclaimed Lilly, and Max nodded in agreement.

The music swelled with the performance, and Calce seemed to be soaring on the waves of the notes until the grand finale. Jumping with all four legs into the air and kicking his hind legs out into the air behind him, the majestic horse performed the *capriole* for the spectators sitting high above.

Mr. Fuchs beamed at them, took a deep bow, and exited with Calce prancing next to him, while the ends of his mustache twirled and winked as erect as none of the siblings had seen it before.

The magnificent performance left everyone in the stands breathless. Celia knew that she would treasure this moment forever in her memories. She clapped and cheered until her hands and voice were sore and then dreamily made her way back to their guest apartment.

Now that the horses were dancing

again, their visit at the Spanish Riding School had ended. It was time to pack their bags and return home to new patients awaiting her parents' help.

The final goodbyes were said, promises of keeping in touch given, and the Cook siblings were just about to climb into their airport taxi when Max gathered the three of them close one more time.

"Together with my classmates in school, I'll be starting a petition to reduce traffic levels in this area," he said proudly. "I'm sure we can convince the town council to make some changes around here, even without talking about the secret voices of our four horses." His dark eyes sparkled with joy.

Celia and Lilly high-fived Max in agreement, while Fynn, as usual, had to have the final word. "Well, I'm not sure they would have appreciated hearing the famous mare of the Lipizzaner bloodline, Pluto Austria, calling them smelly creatures anyway!" He chuckled before waving his last goodbye to their new Austrian friend.

Little did he know that a new adventure for him and his sisters was only a phone call away...

"I understand, yes... the llamas, you say? Ahem... they simply disappeared from the mountains? Of course. Yes. What a disaster!" Mrs. Cook covered her cell phone and turned around to face her children in the backseat of the airport taxi.

"Well, kids, don't unpack your bags just yet. It looks like we are heading to South America... to Peru!"

GLOSSARY

Vienna, Austria: Austria is a small country in the heart of Europe. The city of Vienna, Austria's capital, lies in the country's east on the Danube River. It has a proud history of artists and great minds. Its former residents include Wolfgang Amadeus Mozart, Ludwig van Beethoven, and Sigmund Freud. The city is also known for its imperial palaces, including Schoenbrunn, which has Europe's oldest zoo on its grounds.

The Spanish Riding School: In 1729, Emperor Charles VI commissioned the magnificent Winter Riding School in the Hofburg Palace in Vienna, Austria. It was completed in 1735 and remains in use today. The world-famous Spanish Riding School showcases highly trained Lipizzaner stallions in public performances that demonstrate classical dressage movements and training. There are tours of the stables and tickets to morning training as well as performances available to the public.

Mare: An adult female horse. A *filly* is a female foal up to about four years of age.

Stallion: An adult male horse. A *colt* is a male foal up to about four years of age.

Lipizzaner/Lipizzan: A gray horse breed associated with the Spanish Riding School in Vienna, Austria. It is a compact, muscular horse that is born dark and becomes lighter each year, until between six and ten years of age.

Eight stallions from the late 18th and early 19th centuries are recognized as the foundation bloodstock for this breed. The Sire Lines and Mare Families in this book feature the famous lineages of Pluto, Conversano, Maestoso, Neapolitano. Stallions traditionally are given two names, with the first being the line of the father (sire) and the second being the name of the mother (dam).

Haute École (High School): During this advanced form of classical dressage, the rider brings his horse to perform in perfection. The stallions learn the piaffe, the passage, pirouettes, and to canter in both directions using different lead legs.

The piaffe: A movement where the horse is trotting in place or nearly in place.

The passage: Here the horse performs an extremely powerful trot.

The pirouette: A movement in which the animal makes a circle with its front end around a smaller circle made by the hind end.

It takes approximately six years for a stallion to be ready to take part in the School Quadrille, which officially completes his schooling. Only very few, talented and sensitive stallions master the art of the "schools above the ground" (levade, courbette, capriole).

The levade: A position where the horse raises up both front legs, standing at a thirty-degree angle entirely on its hind legs. This requires a great deal of hindquarter strength.

The courbette: A movement where the horse balances on its hind legs and then „hops," jumping with the forelegs off the ground and hind legs together.

The capriole: A jump in place where the stallion leaps into the air, tucking his forelegs under himself, and kicks out with his hind legs at the top of the jump.

Eleve (Pl. Eleves): French for "pupil," "scholar."

This term is used at the Spanish Riding School for the young, inexperienced riders joining the school on their journey to become fully qualified Riders, or even Chief Riders.

Wolfgang Amadeus Mozart: The composer was born in 1756 in Austria. He developed extraordinary musical abilities, composing and performing in front of royalty from the age of five. Throughout his life, Mozart composed more than six hundred works and remains one of the most recognized and beloved classical composers even today.

The Requiem: W.A. Mozart began composing this musical masterpiece in Vienna shortly before his death in 1791. It remained unfinished by him and was later completed by several other composers.

Sacher Torte: Vienna's most famous dessert is a two-layered chocolate cake filled with apricot jam and covered with dark chocolate icing. It was invented by Franz Sacher, a kitchen boy at that time, in 1832 to be served for a prince.

Michaeler Kirche: St. Michael's Church is one of the oldest churches in Vienna; it is believed to have been built around 1220. It is home to the largest baroque pipe organ in Vienna, which was once played by another famous composer named Joseph Haydn when he was only seventeen years old. Mozart's very last musical piece, *Requiem,* was performed for the first time in this church at a memorial service for the composer on December 10, 1791.

Guten Tag: German for "Hello!" Literally, "Good Day!"

Wunderbar: German for "wonderful."

ABOUT THE AUTHOR

Dori Marx grew up in Austria and tried her best to travel the world several times before choosing gorgeous New England as her home. Here, she lives with her husband, three children, senior dog, three rescue goats, along with an ever-growing number of pet chickens and fish. Although she is not a veterinarian, she has a soft spot for all living beings and has even learned to coexist with the spiders populating her basement.

Wonder World Kids, The Mystery of the Dancing Horses is her first book.

Made in the USA
Middletown, DE
10 January 2020

82961838R00102